The Birth

The Birth

GENE EDWARDS

Copyright
MCMXC
by
Gene Edwards
All Rights Reserved

Published by
The Seed Sowers
Box 3368
Auburn, Maine 04210
ISBN 0-940-232-39-1

*I shall drink from waters deeper than the
spring,
And from the poet's eye shall I read his
book.
But, oh, what I might learn should I dare to
look
From God's view even of the simplest
thing.*

—Christian Maynell

Prologue

Michael first became aware that something momentous was about to take place when he felt a strange compulsion to visit the place of the Door. It was not an area of the heavenlies that angels often frequented.

"Why am I here?" he mused to himself. "Why am I standing at the passageway to the physical realm?" It had been ages since the Door had opened into that realm. Not since Malachi, the prophet, had there been commerce between the two creations.

"Why," the archangel wondered, "has it been so very long since the most high God has spoken face to face with anyone living upon the earthen ball."

At that moment Michael felt a deeper inner stirring. His eyes brightened. He was being called to the Throne. But more. Michael knew, by some inexplicable intuition, that the passageway between heaven and earth would open again, and soon.

"The voice of our Lord will be heard again in realms visible," he whispered, as he turned toward the very center of heavenly places.

What was first felt in Michael's bosom as a quiet sense soon became a strong excitation felt by all the inhabitants of the celestial realm. It would be only a few moments now, and the entire heavenly host would know an event of immeasurable proportions was about to come to pass. Whatever this phenomenon, it was quite clear that it would be the greatest event since creation itself.

1

"Has the enemy asked for an audience?" wondered Michael as his hand moved instinctively to his sword. "Not likely. This summons to the Throne must have to do with the Door and a coming visitation to earth."

As Michael drew near to the throne room, his path led him past Recorder, the most ancient of all the angelic host. Recorder had been created an instant before all other angelic beings so that he might witness and then record all events.

"I have been summoned to the Throne, Recorder."

"Yes, I know," responded the ancient being with a certainty bequeathed only to this most venerable of the angels.

"For what have I been summoned?" asked Michael.

"It has not been given me to know. But that something is about to happen that is quite awesome is a certainty."

"Do you know what this momentous thing will be?" Michael asked.

"Whatever it may be, I know only this: It will change everything."

The archangel considered Recorder's reply for a moment, then moved toward the throne room, there to disappear into the outer edges of unapproachable light. In a moment Michael would find himself in the vortex of glory.

2

"Michael, I have a mission for you." The voice of Almighty God, so familiar to the archangel yet so wondrous to hear, sent a gentle trembling through Michael's spirit.

The mission concerns a prayer. There is a petition being offered up to me from earth, a prayer of the highest possible import. But the passing of that prayer from earth to my Throne has been hindered. Are you aware, Michael, of the hindrance?"

"Yes, Lord, I know. . . ." Michael paused and was about to state what he knew of this "hindrance," but his Lord continued.

"A long time has passed since I have spoken to anyone upon the favored planet. You know that the Door has not opened for many an age."

Michael nodded as every sinew in his being grew taut with anticipation.

"Above the planet, the skies have turned to brass. This has happened but once before, as you well know. It was long ago that I called on you, as I do now, to open a way through the brass. On that former occasion, against all odds, you opened a way from heaven to earth. But be warned, this time the enemy will resist you with even greater fury."

The living God paused and spoke slowly, "The enemy will resist you . . . as never before."

Michael drew his sword, his eyes swarmed with light. "With all eagerness and anticipation I await your word, my Lord!"

"Then go, Michael. Open a pathway from the heavens to the earth. Allow that prayer which is being offered up even now to find its way to my Throne. Gabriel will accompany you. Once a way through the brass is opened, Gabriel has a message to deliver to a priest in Jerusalem. But until such time as the barrier is breached, Gabriel will but stand behind you. It is given to you alone to clear a way to earth."

"Something momentous is about to occur, Lord?" asked Michael.

"It is."

"And the angelic hosts, may I inform them?"

"They already know."

"They know? Lord, what is it that we know?"

"That it is the *fulness of time.*"

Michael raised himself to his full height. *The fulness of time . . . something* he had always known but did not yet understand. Majestically Michael moved his sword above his head and drew near to the presence of his Lord until both he and his sword glistened like white fire. For one brief moment the very glory of God saturated Michael.

Michael stepped back and turned to go. There was a moment's pause. Once more he faced the Throne.

"The skies of brass will be violated," he said matter-of-factly. Then after a moment of reflection, he roared, "A way will be opened!"

The Lord gave a most unexpected reply to Michael's cry. "Breach the sky of brass, Michael, and breach it well, for never again will the skies above the earth be allowed to turn to brass. Never again will the enemy be permitted to erect a blockade between heaven and earth."

Michael trembled from head to foot, and with sword still raised, turned and cried one glad word.

"Gabriel!"

3

The two archangels approached that mysterious place, the sealed and silent Door. There, the two creatures of light waited. After a long moment the ancient portal began to open. Hurriedly Michael sheathed his sword. This was the one place in all the universe he dare not show force, for just beyond the Door stood creatures that not even archangels dared challenge.

Michael was the first to catch sight of the mighty cherubim. Both archangels trembled at the sight of these guardians of the Door. Ever since the Great Tragedy these fierce beings had stood just outside the Door as protectors of the entrance to the heavenly realm. And as if their presence alone were not enough, before them whirled a sword of fire and wrath.

The creatures turned to face the archangels. The

circling, whirling sword slowed, the flame dimmed slightly.

The cherubim stepped back. The Door lay open and unprotected. Michael moved onto the threshold of the Door, his eyes staring straight ahead to avoid even a glimpse of the faces of these creatures of terror.

Having passed the cherubim, the two archangels surveyed the scene that lay before them. They could barely make out the favored planet. A slight groan rose from within the depths of Michael. Truly, the skies above the blue-green planet had turned to brass.

"It was to be expected," sighed Michael. "It has been so long, and our enemy has not been idle. He has gained full control of the skies above the earth."

The Door began to move, then came to rest upon the brass shield. Slowly and purposefully Michael unsheathed his mighty sword and stepped out upon the cold barrier.

"Gabriel, as I advance, and advance I will, stand just behind me until such time as you see the green of earth come into view. The Door will follow us. When I have made a way from our realm to earth, the prayers of men will once more rise unhindered to the ears of God. And you, Gabriel, will once more announce the will of God upon the favored planet."

"Make haste, Michael," replied Gabriel, "for there is one prayer, above all others, that *must* get through."

Michael moved farther out upon the floor of brass and in all deliberation cried out: "Hear me, for I am Michael. Damned, doomed enemy . . . come! Face me in battle!"

For a moment he stood motionless, his sword clasped in both hands. Then slowly, he raised the butt of his sword above his head and rammed the blade hard into the brass.

Once again he raised the sword's handle, and once again he plunged its point into the hardened shield.

Under the bludgeonings of Michael's powerful thrusts the barrier ripped open. Light shot through darkness. From somewhere below screams pierced the air.

The creature who bore the name Michael had just declared a one-angel war against all the powers of darkness!

4

Again and again the sword pierced the brass. Light flooded the black void. Below, creatures of the darkness could be seen forming a first line of defense, but not before Michael had ripped a gaping hole into their domain.

Now Michael boldly stepped into that realm which was claimed by his enemy. Shrieks of anger and cries of fear rose out of the belly of the darkness, but Michael's sword continued to slash and rip as the forces of the enemy fell back in disarray against his relentless assault.

The Door followed hard on Michael's advance. The barrier that stood between earth and the heavenlies was crumbling before his bludgeonings. Unquenchable rays of light swarmed into the blackness.

Suddenly a voice rose from the innermost depth of that dark domain.

"Fools! How dare you fall back? There is no power to equal mine. No creature dare assault my kingdom. None can conquer here. What fool has dared enter *my* realm?"

It was the enraged voice of the captain of the damned, the voice Michael craved to hear. Pulling back his sword far to the right of his shoulder, Michael plunged it hard into the shroud of darkness.

The two archangels came face to face.

"You! Michael! How dare you! What arrogant madness brings you here? Do you not know me?" he shrieked, his fists raised above his head. "I am the angel of light. In every way I am your superior."

"No," snarled Michael. "Damned, doomed Lucifer, begetter of all lies, traitor of the angelic host, counterfeiter of truth and elected to eternal damnation, you are in every way my equal, but you are in no way my superior. Stand aside, damned foe, for I am on a mission from the Holiest of All."

Lucifer's eyes danced passed Michael.

"No!" screamed the fallen archangel. "Not the Door! Not here. Not in my kingdom. You, Michael, with your cursed power, and you, Gabriel, with your damnable heraldings . . . never,

never shall you pass beyond this point." Gleaming with dark rage, Lucifer reached for his sword. This was the moment around which lay all Michael's strategy.

> You spawn of Hell,
> You kin of sin,
> You only friend of fiend
> Azell.
> Step aside, incarnate
> pride.
>
> One day,
> Outside of time and
> eternity,
> It was the lot that fell to
> me
> To drive you into that place
> for which you are
> fit.
> I, Michael,
> shall cast you into the
> smoking,
> blazing,
> fiery
> pit!
>
> Now draw your sword, or find full
> well
> That even now I'll send you to eternal
> Hell!

Just as Michael had hoped, Lucifer went into a blind rage even as he grappled wildly for his sword.

"Stand aside, you spawn of hell," cried Michael.

With that, all sounds knelt to silence. Every eye

now turned to watch two archangels about to be welded in unbridled combat.

The radiance of both archangels rose in brilliance, Michael's light giving off glowing rays of whitened purity, Lucifer's vestige bursting forth in unparalleled brightness, flashing in tones of blue.

Both beings pulled back their swords to the limits of their reach, then whirled in full circle, Michael to the right, Lucifer to the left. And as their swords met full on with all the strength bequeathed these two celestial creatures, a sound of a thousand thunders reverberated across the length and breadth of both realms.

Light and darkness had come to the pinnacle of their purposes . . . each to destroy the other.

5

The two archangels thrusted and parried, then whirling about, crashed their swords one against the other. Again and again the weapons clanged like discordant bells, while a chant of dark screams rose and fell in demonic chorus.

Little by little the angel of light gave way under Michael's devastating blows. On and on Michael pressed the battle, and as he did, the Door advanced with him, while Gabriel, silent and still, stood upon its threshold and waited.

Michael had at last driven Lucifer back to the very edge of his dark domain. Just beyond lay earth. The victory seemed certain. Heaven and earth would once more touch, and commerce would once again be known between the two realms.

Lucifer paused, his eyes flashing blue-white, his

whole vesture pouring forth blinding light. Raising his sword with wicked glee, he declared what Michael wished least to hear, but which he surely could not deny.

"This is as far as you can go, Michael, for here you stand in *my* kingdom. You have no authority to drive me out. By decree, the skies are mine. You have come this far, but you will go no further."

Michael knew that what the fallen archangel had spoken was indeed true. For a moment Michael wrestled within himself, seeking to discover his next move.

"I have a mission to perform," he said to himself. "The most high God has sent me as an envoy to earth. I must pass beyond this spot." Suddenly within his spirit the answer came, as Michael recalled a word that he had spoken to Lucifer in ages long past.

Gabriel stood dumbfounded as he watched Michael not only lower his sword in the presence of his archenemy, but beyond all belief, even sheath his weapon. Was this defeat? Surely Michael, of all creatures, had not given up! Gabriel watched, motionless, as Michael raised himself to his full height, his raiment glowing pure white. Lighted by liquid rage, Michael stepped forward, well into the range of Lucifer's sword, and then thundered his reply.

"For once you have spoken that which is true. I have no authority to drive you from this domain, for it was given you by the most high God when you were thrust out of the spiritual realm long ago. I cannot, therefore, in that way order you. Nor can I rebuke you. But there is One who can.

"In the name of the most high and living God, you are rebuked, Lucifer. Step out of my path! Begone! In the name of my Lord and yours, you are rebuked."

A hell-chilling scream rose from Lucifer's throat. His light shone white, then blue, and then flared into a flaming black. The chorus of demonic wails subsided.

Lucifer vanished with the wails.

Michael unsheathed his sword and hurled one last blow against the wall of brass. The shield collapsed. Michael had slain the dark. The blue-green of earth lay just beyond.

Suddenly, the Door moved, and came to rest within a sparsely furnished room. From somewhere in the shadows a prayer could be heard. It was a woman's voice. As she spoke, her prayer passed through the Door and at last ascended unhindered to the very Throne of God.

> "Lord, take away my shame. Though I am past the years of a fruitful womb, hear my prayer. Give me a child. A son. Give him to me and I will give him back to you for your purpose . . . for the accomplishment of your will upon the earth."

This time, it was Gabriel who stepped forward.

Quietly, gently, he spoke to the gray-haired woman kneeling beside her bed.

"Hail, Elizabeth! The prayer you have offered to your God has been answered. Your Lord has taken notice of you and has removed your reproach in the eyes of men. You shall bear a son."

6

The most sacred offering of the day was about to be offered. It was a high hour for the priests as they cast lots to choose who would go alone into the Holy Place and there make the sacred offering. No priest who had ever done so before was eligible to be chosen again. Those who had never made this offering waited in anticipation of the results.

Today the lot fell to the oldest priest present, a man named Zachariah. As his name was announced, one of the other priests knelt beside him and tied a rope around his ankle. Should Zachariah see the face of God while he was in the Holy Place, he would surely die. The rope would then serve as the one way his body could be recovered.

Zachariah stood before the entrance to the temple both terrified and expectant. Slowly he entered the Holy Place, studied this mysterious room, and then began to perform the ancient rituals of his ancient faith.

Little did Zachariah realize as he went about his priestly task that at this moment the Door between the two realms had moved from his very home where his wife, Elizabeth, had just received a heavenly visitation, and had come to rest within that part of the temple where he now stood. From out of the other realm Gabriel stepped into this sacred room. Zachariah, becoming aware that someone stood behind him, turned to see what audacious priest had dared follow him into the Holy Place.

But instead of a priest, what Zachariah saw was the most incredible being that human eyes might dare to gaze upon. Before him, standing to the right of the altar of incense, was some kind of shining being from the other realm.

"Who are you?" asked a terrified Zachariah.

But from out of the mouth of the angel came words as reassuring as Zachariah had ever heard.

> "Do not be afraid. I am here to tell you that your prayers for the deliverance of Israel have been heard. Your wife, Elizabeth, will bear a son. When the child is born, you are to name him John. And on the day of his birth you will be joyful and full of gladness.
>
> "There will be many who will rejoice at the birth of your son, for he will grow to be great in the eyes of your Lord. He will not drink wine, nor

any other strong drink, and he will be filled with the Holy Spirit even when he is in his mother's womb.

"Furthermore, many of the people of Israel will be turned to the Lord God because of him, and it will be your son who will go before the Lord. He will go in the spirit and the power of Elijah. He will turn the hearts of the fathers to the children. The disobedient he will turn to the wisdom of righteousness. It will be the task of your son to prepare a people for the Lord when He comes."

Zachariah, dazed in the presence of the glowing angel, began to shake his head. "No, No! That is not possible. No, No! This cannot be. How can I know this is true? Look at me. You see I am an old man. And my wife is past the time of child-bearing."

Gabriel was not accustomed to living in a realm where things that were true were also doubted. He took a step toward Zachariah and glared down at him.

"I am the angel of God. I am the announcer of the will of the Most High. It is I who stand in the very presence of the Lord. It is my God, the almighty God, who sent me here to speak to you. I have brought you glad tidings, and you have not believed. Therefore, you shall be dumb! You will not speak another word until the day these things come to pass. You have not believed my words, but in time my words will be fulfilled."

With that, Gabriel vanished.

"Where has he gone?" marveled Zachariah. "How could he have just disappeared?"

This very confused priest was about to demand the archangel's return, only to discover that he had lost his voice! In horror, Zachariah clutched at his throat with one hand and clawed at the air with the other. He began beating on the golden walls trying to find the secret passageway by which the angel had so suddenly departed. His efforts were futile, for the creature whom he so desperately sought was now a universe away.

Finally Zachariah ran, most unceremoniously, out of the Holy Place and into the courtyard, all the while pointing at his throat with both his hands. Seeing that no one understood him, he pointed to his eyes, gesturing frantically, trying to describe with his hands the lighted creature he had just seen. All in all, he did no more than make himself a spectacle before the waiting throng. His gestures were unclear but the message was obvious. Zachariah had seen some sort of vision within the Temple and had been struck dumb by the sight of it.

7

This was the first time in all angelic memory that the most high God had come to the passageway between the two worlds. Gabriel alone accompanied Him.

"The fulness of time has arrived," said the Lord. "What you are about to do is no less than to begin revealing *the Mystery*. My eternal Purpose, the purpose for which I created the worlds, is about to be made known. Be sure, Gabriel, no mind has ever conceived nor even dreamed what that Purpose is."

There is little that any angel fears, and certainly even less that might unnerve an archangel. But Gabriel was shaken to the core to learn that *he* would be the one to first herald these tidings.

As the conversation came to an end, Gabriel bowed low before his God. Turning to face the

Door, the angel trembled at the realization of where it would open.

Gabriel hesitated. Almost in angelic embarrassment, he spoke again. On several occasions you have . . . well, to say the least . . . *surprised* the angelic host. That day in Egypt when you challenged the angel of death, Azell; when you revealed to us that on some unknown future day you would be . . . wounded! Then there are those rumors which have been among us almost from the day of our creation. Often we have asked 'Why did He create? What is His ultimate purpose?' My Lord, we have wondered often concerning your purpose. But never before has any creature, even Recorder, ever heard the words, 'my *eternal* Purpose.' An *eternal* purpose, Lord? Eternal? A purpose that reaches far beyond even salvation for mankind? A purpose *before* the Fall, a purpose *before* creation, a purpose that will continue into eternity even after redemption itself is complete? May we dare inquire as to that purpose?"

"A little longer, Gabriel; then you shall know. A little longer . . . and all the host of heaven shall know."

With that, Gabriel turned toward his task. As he stepped onto the threshold of the now open Door, he heard a girl's voice. Whoever she was, she was singing.

8

She was a teenager. She was beautiful. She was also in love. Only a few days ago she had been betrothed to the young man she adored.

Years ago, in her early childhood, this young woman's parents had moved from their home in Judea and resettled in Galilee. Her fiance, a carpenter by trade, had recently moved from the village of Bethlehem to Nazareth, to open a carpentry shop.

These two young people, Mary and Joseph by name, had met at one of the local festivals and had fallen in love. Soon thereafter, Joseph had gone to both their parents asking for permission to marry. The two families decided that a marriage was permissible, but the date decided upon was nearly a year away. Joseph was poor, they had agreed, his carpentry business just beginning; therefore, wisdom dictated that the two should wait at least a year before marrying.

Now, on this very ordinary day, it was destined that an archangel would pay a visit to this young maiden.

"Mary," came a voice from behind her.

Having never heard a voice quite so commanding, Mary turned quickly about. What she saw caused her to fall to her knees. There was no question in her mind that the creature standing before her belonged to the citizenship of the other realm.

Mary could not imagine what to expect from the mouth of this strange being. Some terrible command? Some awful rebuke? Some prophecy of doom? Perhaps he would smite her with some horrible disease. His words could not have held a more astounding surprise.

> "Mary, you are a very blessed young woman. The Lord Himself is with you."

Mary's eyes darted about as she tried to grasp what these words might mean.

> "You do not need to be afraid. Among all the women who have dwelt upon this earth since Eve, you are the most favored. You are going to conceive a child in your womb. You will bring forth a son. His name will be Jesus. He will be

called the son of the most high God, and He will be great.

> "The throne of His ancestor, David, will be given to your son by the Lord God Himself. He will reign forever and forever. The kingdom of your son will never end."

"I . . . I . . ." Mary stammered. "I do not understand! I am a virgin! I have never touched a man, nor has any man touched me. And my betrothed, it will be a long time before we shall marry."

Mary's words met with a long silence, and Mary did not like that. She dared, therefore, to lift her head and look up at this fearsome-looking creature standing before her. To her surprise, what she saw on his face was kindness and gentleness. But more. He seemed to be somewhat awe-struck himself. For one fleeting moment she sensed that the angel beheld her with as much wonder as she did him.

Seeing the gentleness upon the face of this unearthly being, Mary began to feel a deep sense of courage fill her heart. Drawing upon that courage, she dared rise to her feet and look directly into the eyes of the archangel. She waited.

At last Gabriel spoke.

> "It will be no man; it will be the Holy Spirit. He will come upon you. The power of the most high God will overshadow you. That which will be conceived in you, the holy thing that will be born

from you, will be called the Son of God. Even now your cousin, Elizabeth, though she is old and past the age of motherhood, has, nonetheless, conceived a son. Elizabeth, who was barren, is now already six months with child."

Mary's eyes widened. What she had heard concerning herself was beyond all understanding, but hearing that Elizabeth was also about to bear a child seemed even more astounding.

Gabriel turned to go, as is the way of angels when they have finished their task. But on this occasion he paused for a moment to stand once more in awe of the young woman chosen to bring Almighty God into humanity's realm.

"A mere woman," he mused, incredulous. "A *human* being."

Aloud, he said, "It seems that there is absolutely nothing impossible with our God."

Stepping back toward the Door, Gabriel was stopped short as Mary boldly advanced toward him. He could not recall having ever seen such a show of human boldness in the presence of an angel. Furthermore, this time it was Mary who had a pronouncement to make. She spoke with such passion that Gabriel was, for an instant, taken aback.

"Behold, I stand here, the handmaiden of my Lord. The words that you have spoken I receive. Let what you have said be done unto me."

Within the glow of that angelic presence Mary thought she might have seen a soft smile cross Gabriel's face.

With this mutually unprecedented encounter, Gabriel stepped onto the threshold of the Door. As he did, he whispered to himself, "Truly, our God has chosen well."

9

Only the cherubim saw the Living God pass through the Door and into the visible realm, there to freely wander the corridors of time.

The Lord raised His hand, and suddenly the ancient past appeared. The Lord stepped into the Garden of Eden.

The beauty of the Garden was breathtaking. For a few moments He roamed its floral wonders, its verdant meadows. He breathed the purity of the air of that bygone era as it had existed before the planet had fallen. Finally, He paused and spoke to the Garden.

"Once the glories of earth and the glories of heaven met and joined here. The best of both realms touched, and you, oh, Garden, were the meeting place. It was here, primordial Garden, that angels played together, and all the joys of earth and heaven were *one*. Then came that tragic day. It was necessary that I seal off the heavenlies from the earth. Man was cast out of you, and angels returned to their own realm. You, oh, Garden, disappeared from view.

"But my purpose was not thwarted! I will yet join the highest glory of heaven with the highest that earth affords. And I will do so in the coming hour! But on *this* occasion, it will not be you, a garden, that will gather the two realities into one. *I* shall be the joining. I, the Light of the heavenlies, will become *Man*.

I, a man of earth, and I, the God of heaven . . . *I* will be the coming together of the highest of two realms. *I* will be the oneness."

The Living God raised His hand again, and yet another scene from the ancient past appeared. The Lord now stood before some mound . . . a sculpting of clay. The clay began to stir. Dirt was becoming a living being. Indeed, clay was becoming a man!

The Lord watched as the glowing sculpture trembled in its change from humus to human, from soil to soul. The Lord knelt beside the naked creature and spoke.

"Man, once *you* were the joining of two realms. I formed you out of the very elements of this planet's sod, but then I gave you a spirit which came from the very heavenlies. You were, therefore, a creature composed of elements from both realms. The two creations joined within your bosom. A *man* made two realms . . . one.

"Alas, fair creature, the bond did not hold, for the last ingredient you needed, the highest element of the heavenlies, was never added to you. *My* life in you. You chose not to partake of *my* life. What tragedy that you refused to take my life into you. And there followed hard on a tragedy as equally great. You fell. You so dreadfully fell. But that fall did *not* thwart my purpose . . . My e*ternal Purpose.*

"The fulness of time is here. *Now.* Today it will not be man who weds the two creations into one. On *this* occasion it will be God. Yes, it will be in the bosom of God Himself that the two creations will join again. The highest of all things in heavenly places and the highest of man's high reaches shall become *one* . . . in me."

The Lord stood and raised His hand. The scene changed once more. What emerged was not something from the ancient past, but the present. The site was an encamped caravan. The hour was late. All had gone to bed except a desert wanderer and a much beleaguered rabbi who had made the mistake of engaging this Bedouin tramp in a religious discussion.

"How can you not believe in God?" exclaimed the rabbi. "Look at all there is around you."

"I did not say I do not believe in God, but only that there is no evidence of Him. I say to you, if

He does exist, He does not work hard at letting us know it. There is even less evidence that He cares for us."

"But the Scripture says . . ." sputtered the rabbi.

"The Scripture! Forget what is written. If there is a God, then let Him come down here where we are. Let Him live in this filthy place where we live. Let Him smell the stink, let Him feel the poverty, let Him know pain, let Him see the hunger . . . let Him *feel* the hunger. Let Him know what it is to eek out an existence in wretched poverty. Let Him see a friend die, feel the agony of loss, the unfairness of death. Let Him know what it is to watch a little child die and see it taken from its mother's arms for burial. Let Him see our diseases, the sockets of blind eyes, the twisted feet. Let this God of yours be hated, jeered, cheated, and robbed. Let Him lose everything He owns at the hands of the wicked. Let Him be dragged before a court of law, as was I. Let Him discover firsthand how unjust justice really is!"

The Bedouin's vehemence grew as he continued. "And sin! He is so interested in whether or not I sin; let Him feel my temptation. Let Him experience *my* weaknesses. Then let us see how He feels about all the rules and commands He has put on *me*— rules I cannot live up to, yet if I do not live up to them, He will not like me anymore!

"Let Him feel what I feel, here in this miserable

aching, decaying body of mine! And then, *let Him die!* Yes, let Him die the way I will probably die, like most wanderers die, out here *alone.* Homeless, uncared for, forsaken, forgotten! If He wants to impress me, let Him become like me. Then maybe I will believe in your God . . . but not until then!"

Though the Bedouin did not hear, he, nonetheless, was given a most astounding reply.

"Bedouin," said the Lord, " You are wiser than you know. Yes, *far* wiser than you know."

The Lord was about to step back into time's corridors, but paused instead and addressed the desert wanderer once more.

"And, Bedouin, we shall meet again, on a high hill. And together we shall die." He paused again. "And together we shall rise!

"Now I must go, for the hour has come for me to become one with my creation."

The Lord raised His hand once more. This time He lifted off the planet and rose high above the clouds. For a moment He paused midway between the two realms and viewed the fallen creation.

"My enemy! Sin! Death!" He cried. "You have had your short day! Soon those whom I will redeem shall become one with me. Your frail efforts to thwart my Purpose will end. My ultimate reason for creation, to gather my chosen ones and make them one with me, has *never* been in jeopardy.

"Soon I will come for those I have chosen . . . in a way that will astound even the angels. Soon I will begin to bridge the chasm that keeps us apart.

Divinity and humanity . . . one . . . in me. I will walk the earth. I will live in my creation. I will become visible, for *all* to see. Nothing now living, or that has ever lived, has seen what is about to be: One who is wholly man and wholly divine."

With that, the Lord called across the universe. "Come time, come eternity, come spirituals, come physicals, lose your separation and meet in me! Now beyond all thought of man and wildest dream of angels, *now* to my *eternal Purpose.*"

As He stepped back through the open Door, the most high God called out one word.

"Recorder!"

10

The entire angelic throng had gathered, swarming in a vast circle around the most ancient of all the angels. Anticipation hung thick in the air. Whatever it was Recorder had to tell them, they knew for a certainty it was unprecedented. The fact that it was Recorder and not Gabriel making this pronouncement was in itself unique.

"What I have to announce to you is not something I fully understand," began Recorder. "What you hear *you* will not entirely grasp. None of us will ever fully know what is taking place this hour. But this much can be said: Creation has entered into a new era. The very *Purpose* for which the living God created our two realms is now unfolding. This hour will forever mark the moment when our Lord began to reveal the *Mystery*."

The word "Purpose" slipped past the angels, but when Recorder uttered the word "Mystery," an angel-wide gasp swept through the multitude. Rumors of some undisclosed wonder had been whispered among the heavenly citizens almost since the moment of their creation.

"And what is it that we are about to see," Recorder continued, "I am not sure. As best I can, I share with you what the living God has shared with me.

"There is something of the very life and essence of the Father, the very inmost portion of His being, which is about to . . . "

Recorder paused. Had the light of the heavenlies . . . blinked? Yes, something about the heavenly light, for one brief moment, had been altered.

There was a long silence. Then Recorder spoke again.

"Momentarily there will take place the greatest event ever to be known in all the history of creation."

It happened again, some imperceptible change in the light that lighted heaven.

One of the angels turned in the direction of the Throne of God. What he saw was ineffable. In a moment the eyes of all the angelic host had turned in the same direction.

The Throne and the Door, for the first time ever, had drawn together. And, at the same moment, the very light of the life of God was enfolding itself into one brilliant, but one very small, area just in front of the Door.

Angels watched in astonishment as the tiny light grew more intense. So bright became this concentration of light that angels, who are able to look even into the very face of God, now stood blinded by this brilliance.

"It is as though all the light of the spirituals is gathering into one infinitesimal place," thought Michael, as he raised his hand to shield his eyes.

Now the Door between the two realms opened again. The cherubim, whose faces had brought fear to even archangels, now stood transfixed in terror.

The entire angelic host, still blinded by this infinitely bright light, intuitively moved toward the Door. Could it be that something of the very essence and totality of God was about to pass into the other realm?

In the midst of this incomprehensible moment, the voice of Recorder was heard once again.

"Many of us have passed through this portal that joins our two realms. Long ago, as you recall, the Door was always open. The two realms joined together . . . at a place called Eden. After the Great Tragedy, the Door closed.

"On infrequent occasions, at the command of our God, the Door has opened. Several times the Lord stepped through this Door to visit **Abraham**. Once this Door opened for Moses and the seventy elders to step into our realm. Once also for Isaiah, who stood in this very doorway and looked upon our dwelling place. But always the Door has closed again. Michael and Gabriel have recently made passage through the Door to the home of Elizabeth, and again into that replica of the Holy of Holies in Jerusalem to speak face to face with Zachariah. But never before has anything such as this occurred.

"Today, the Door opens inside a woman's womb!"

At that very instant the dazzling concentration of light plunged through the open Door and into the visible realm.

Stupefied angels, utterly without a single insight as to what had just happened, turned back to face Recorder and to wonder at what it was Gabriel and Michael had made possible by their recent visit to earth.

11

"Do you not understand?" cried Recorder to a host of blank- faced angels. That the stately and reserved Recorder was quite beside himself was enough to unnerve any angel, but the significance of his pronouncement to these creatures of revelation was entirely beyond their reach.

"Have you not understood?" Recorder cried again. "Among the children of Adam, a virgin has at this moment conceived!"

Every mouth of every angel dropped open, every eye blinked, and every throat swallowed.

"At this moment there grows One, in a woman's womb, who carries with Him all that is the highest, the purest, and the greatest innocence . . . all the grandeur of an Adam *before* the Fall. And at this moment, growing inside that same womb, is the very life of God. There shall come forth from this virgin womb the highest of unfallen mankind, the very Son of Man . . . Himself. And from this womb shall come forth all the essence of God, the very Son of God. The two at last have met in One, and His name shall be called Jesus, for He shall save mankind from the ravages that sin has wreaked upon their race.

"But even this is but for a greater end. As He, this day, has made Himself one with them, there shall come an hour when those chosen by Him for redemption will, in greater glory, be made one with Him."

Millions of dumbfounded angels continued to gape at the ancient Recorder.

"Do you not understand?" he cried. "Redemption is near! Salvation for the favored planet is at hand. And beyond our wildest dreams, The Mystery will soon be known. His Purpose . . . the *eternal* Purpose . . . His reason for creation will soon be revealed. We stand at the highest moment in all eternal history."

The stunned silence was broken by Michael who had spontaneously whirled about to find his closest kinsman. "Gabriel!" he exclaimed. "Did you know these things would be the final outcome of all we have been doing of late?"

"No!" cried Gabriel. "Did you?"

"Never!" Michael answered. "Oh, that we have played a part in such glory."

Michael drew his sword, raised his arms high, threw back his head, and deafened the heavenly host as he roared (as only Michael can), "Redemption draweth nigh!" To which Gabriel responded, "The Mystery revealed, the Purpose made known!"

And so it came to pass that for the first of only two times in all the history of "angelicdom," chaos descended upon the heavenly host, and to the delight of innumerable beings of light, all order broke down, bedlam reigned, and frolicking angels shouted themselves hoarse.

12

Every son and daughter of Adam ever born has been born of the *seed* of man, the mutated chromosome of the male forever passing on to Adam's race the damning legacy of the Fall.

Yet long ago, in the first book of Moses, it had been foretold that once, and only once, a man-child would be born of the seed of a woman.[*] And it would be this son of a woman's seed who would destroy the enemy of God.

And so it came to pass that once, and only once, a man child was born of the seed of woman.

And the woman's name was Mary.

While Mary slept, the Holy Spirit overshadowed this young maiden, and the seed of woman sprang

---

[*]Genesis 3:15

into germination. And in this wondrous seed there was *none* of the sin-stained DNA of the descendants of the man Adam.

So from Mary's exotic seed there began to form a soul and body unscarred by the history of fallen man.

In that same mysterious moment, an even greater wonder emerged, for the very *DNA of God* joined with this unique seed. And so there joined in this one-cell embryo an unblemished body and soul from the visible realm. And from the invisible realm there was joined to this embryo a living spirit . . . even the very spirit and life of God.

The very essence of all that God is pulsated deep within that man-child embryo. Behold, the genetics of unfallen mankind growing together with the genetics of God.

Residing within these now multiplying cells was a truly *living* human spirit. Surely nothing like this had existed since Adam's spirit flickered out in the garden and Adam died to the spiritual realm.

And thus it came about that there was conceived, once, and only once, One who was wholly Son of Man and wholly Son of God.

Earth had never witnessed such a conception. Sinless man, with the very life of God the Father dwelling within. Heaven had never witnessed such a conception: almighty God . . . become visible in human form, in the physical realm.

What grew in Mary's womb was a being unlike any creature that had ever existed before. Would He remain unique, a glorious one-of-a-kind, or did He portend the beginning of a new species?

Whatever this One was, whatever He would become, His conception was quite simply the greatest single miracle of all time.

For in that hour, God became a Man!

13

The carpenter smashed his mallet hard upon the table, picked it up again and threw it against the wall. Then he turned and kicked at the door until his foot was numb. Circling the room in a dance of madness, the young man came at last to the center of the room, placed his hands over his ears, threw back his head, and screamed to the top of his voice. When he could do that no longer, Joseph dropped to the floor, buried his face in the sawdust, and wept uncontrollably.

He raised his head, and between dry lips, cried, "Mary, Mary, how could you do this? Of all the women upon the face of the earth! *You* of all people! How could you do this?"

Once more Joseph clenched his fists and, as in some ceremonial cadence, began beating upon the floor.

"Everything about her said she loved her Lord," the young man anguished. "She was the purest thing I have ever known. If Mary cannot be trusted, then no man can trust any woman who ever lived!"

He stood and cried out again. "How could she do this? It is inconceivable. How? How?" The sobs exploded from Joseph's soul. "I will never marry her. I will never marry *anyone*. I will never trust another woman. Never!"

Emotionally spent, and on the edge of exhaustion, the young carpenter fell once more to the floor and cried himself to sleep.

At that moment, the Door swung open. Gabriel slipped through the portal, surveyed the destruction Joseph had inflicted upon his wood shop, and then, tenderly, knelt beside the young man who was lost in fitful sleep.

"Son of David. Joseph. Do not be afraid. Take Mary as your wife. The child was conceived of the Holy Spirit. When He is born, call His name Jesus. This is that One who will save His people from their sins."

Joseph moved slightly, let out a long sigh, and began to breathe evenly. The agonizing groans that had been rising from his throat ceased. Gently Gabriel laid his hand upon Joseph's forehead and waited—waited until his sleep flowed evenly and peace had worked its way across his face.

Then Gabriel spoke again.

"Our God has well chosen the man who will raise the very Son of the most high God. And, Joseph, as you will learn in the days and years to come, God has also well chosen His mother . . . and your wife."

With that, Gabriel slipped back through the Door and into his own realm. Joseph opened his eyes. What he saw was a room . . . no, an entire world, quite changed from what it had been just a few hours earlier.

14

"Mary! We have been married only, uh, less than . . . less than a month! And you are going to leave me for three months? You cannot be serious!"

"Elizabeth needs me. She is not young. And when I was a child Elizabeth was my closest and dearest friend. Joseph, women her age do not bear children. She needs my help."

"Mary, this is pure madness."

"Joseph, I must do it."

"You must not, you may not, you cannot, and you will not."

Mary folded her arms in a gesture of defiance, her lower lip protruding ever so slightly but quite firmly.

There was a moment's pause as two wills jousted in silence.

"Alright, go help her. But not three months, Mary. I am a working man! From dawn to dark I work. Six days a week, all year long. I need your help—to cook, to clean, to be with me. Mary, not *three months!* You cannot be gone that long."

"Joseph, son of Mathan, I *must* stay with Elizabeth . . . until the day her baby is born. I *will.*"

"And that is another thing, Mary, daughter of Heli— stubborn, strong willed Heli, I am quick to add! *You* are pregnant. You do not need to be going half a country away to look after someone you have not seen in years. You need someone to look after *you*. But oh, no, you are going to trek from here to Judea, alone, on foot, to help someone else have her baby. Well, who is going to take care of *you?* And who is going to take care of *me?*"

Joseph paused, then marshaling even higher logic, continued.

"And furthermore, Elizabeth and Zachariah live in the hill country. What you are proposing is a long, hard journey. Those hills go almost straight up, and the roads in that region are dangerous. In fact, that whole area is dangerous. There are more robbers in those hills than anywhere else in Judea. No one in your condition has any business out there in that kind of country."

There was a long silence. Then Mary spoke, this time soft and low.

"I do not fully understand what has happened to me, Joseph. But I am certain an angel appeared to me; I am certain an angel spoke to you. And you, Joseph, dear husband, so quickly came and married me, which has meant everything to me. Beyond that, there is so little I understand. But this I do know: A child is growing in my belly. I do not fully know who He is, but He is not from this planet. He is from another world. He is from God Himself. I dare not even say what it was the angel called Him.

"And now, this letter, coming from Elizabeth, confirming the words of the angel. Impossible as it is, Elizabeth also has a man-child growing in her womb. Both of these children have been conceived in strange and mysterious ways. Their births, and their lives here on this earth, are inseparably linked, *that* I know. And this I also know I am supposed to go to Elizabeth. And I will. As to dangers, a God who can cause a virgin to conceive can also protect her from hills and highwaymen. Besides, Joseph, you know it is customary for a pregnant woman to seclude herself for a time. Being away in Judea with my pregnant cousin seems so right for now."

With that, Mary sat down upon a bench and

leaned back against the wall. Joseph thought that perhaps, just perhaps, he saw a mischievous smile tugging at the corners of her mouth as she began to speak again.

"And as for you, Jacob Joseph, son of Mathan—stubborn, strong willed Mathan, I might add—you have been taking care of yourself, cooking your own meals, cleaning your house, and tending to your needs long before you met me!"

Joseph breathed a long, slow sigh and relaxed his taut shoulders. Against his will, a slight smile danced across his face.

"Mary, daughter of Heli, I just want you to know that there was never a day in the life of Mathan when he was as stubborn, head strong, or as good at winning an argument as was Heli."

As the eyes of the young couple met, Joseph could no longer keep the smile from blooming on his face. Mary, the woman who both baffled and delighted him, smiled back. Then she leaned over, stifled a giggle, suddenly sat up straight, clapped her hands together and said, "Our very first argument. And I won! Isn't love wonderful!"

15

"Elizabeth?"

"Mary!"

A woman well past middle age ran out of her doorway toward a tired, dust-covered young girl struggling up the narrow limestone street. The two met and embraced. There was an edge of excitement and wonder between them that reached far beyond the ordinary.

"Soon?" Mary asked.

"Only three more months. And you?"

"Six more months. I'm just getting started."

"Yes," nodded Elizabeth, "but your child . . . just now when you called out to me, my son leaped in my womb. He *knew*. It was prophesied that my son would be full of the Holy Spirit even before he was born. And he knew. He leaped! An unborn child knew his Lord! Without sight or sound, he knew. What holy thing is this in you, Mary, that my son has been chosen to recognize Him and precede Him?"

Mary did not, could not, reply.

"Mary! Believe! Believe that the things told you are true, and that they will come to pass."

Elizabeth paused, then added, "You know that I receive you here today as my cousin, and you are so very welcome in our home. But I also receive you in *honor,* as the mother of my very Lord, and the Lord of my yet unborn child."

The teen-age girl pressed a clenched fist hard against her lips, as hot tears began pouring down her cheeks. Tears that betrayed the struggle within her to grasp the magnitude of what had come upon her.

After a quiet moment of struggle Mary turned her face to the west and lifted her eyes skyward toward a setting sun.

She began in a whisper. "I do not . . . I cannot . . . fully understand. But *praise* . . . I will not hold back my praise . . . to You!"

Lifting both hands above her head, Mary cried out, toward the setting sun, the heavens, and an enthroned Lord:

"My God! My Saviour!
My soul magnifies you,

> My spirit rejoices in you.
> You have looked upon this
> simple maiden,
> And from henceforth, now
> and forevermore,
> I will be called blessed.
>
> Oh, Mighty One,
> In me, you have done
> great things.
> Holy is your name.
> Now, and forever,
> from age to age.
> And merciful are you
> to all who revere you.
>
> What a mighty arm is yours!
> You have scattered the proud
> and their vaunted imaginations;
> You have pulled men down
> from their thrones.
> And now you have exalted
> those of low degree;
> You have filled the hungry
> with good things,
> And the rich you have
> sent away empty.
> You have helped
> Your servant Israel,
> And remembered your mercy
> which you promised
> to our fathers,
> To Abraham and
> to his seed
> forever!

For a long time Mary stood there trembling with both relief and joy while fresh tears spilled down her cheeks.

After a moment Elizabeth slipped quietly to Mary's side and gently placed her arm around the young girl's waist. Together they stood there gazing at the blazing sunset until it disappeared below the horizon.

"Now, come inside. And, welcome! You are definitely going to add some spark to this place. How long can you stay?"

"Until your child is born . . . I hope. I do have a problem, though. My Joseph wants me home earlier than that. And though I want very much to obey him, I feel I belong here. But Joseph thinks that at some point I should start acting like an expectant mother."

"I know," laughed Elizabeth. "Zachariah is acting the same way. He has given me much difficulty, that one, and he cannot even talk! We had better stick together, or our men are going to take all the fun out of being pregnant."

16

Kinfolk from all over Judea had made their way to the village of Zachariah and Elizabeth. The neighborhood, too, had become much involved. After all, this was the event of the year! A woman beyond her childbearing age was in labor! Her husband, an old man, a Levite and priest, a man who had seen an angel and who had been struck dumb by that self-same angel, was about to become a father.

This was not an event to be missed.

On this particular morning the entire street around Zachariah's home was filled with friends and onlookers. Just before noon a midwife came to the door and announced to the waiting crowd, "It is a boy. A fine, healthy boy! Zachariah finally has a son."

The child was small, but wiry and strong. His

dark eyes matched his swarthy skin. But his most outstanding feature was an enormous mop of raven-black hair.

One of the midwives gave the child a rubdown in dry salt, bathed him in water, dried him off, and pronounced him whole and healthy. Moments later another of the midwives wrapped the child and brought him to Elizabeth.

"Elizabeth, be proud. He is a fine baby." Then, speaking to the infant, the midwife said, "Here, Zachariah, this is your mother."

"Oh, no," protested Elizabeth. "His name is not Zachariah; his name is John."

Everyone within earshot fell silent. One of the midwives slipped out, made her way into the very crowded living room, and approached Zachariah. "Is your son to be called Zachariah, after you?"

Now how does someone get a clear answer from a man struck dumb? Cautiously, the midwife continued. "Elizabeth says his name is to be John, not Zachariah."

With that, Zachariah began making signs with his hands. Finally in frustration, he motioned for paper. A scribe stepped forward with a small piece of papyrus. Zachariah began to scribble.

> "His name is John."

At that very instant Zachariah dropped the stylus and grabbed at his throat. Everyone gasped.

Several friends rushed to his aid. Just then, a broad smile broke across his face, for a faint squeak had emerged from his throat!

"I can speak. I can talk!" he cried.

A shout of joy went up from everyone in the living room. But in the adjacent room, the newly named John broke out in a squall, while Elizabeth began weeping uncontrollably.

By now Zachariah was standing in the middle of the room shouting hallelujahs at the top of his lungs. Half enraptured, a flood of joy of the Holy Spirit flowed out of him.

> "You are blessed, Lord God
> of Israel!
> You have redeemed your people.
> Out of the house of David
> You have raised up a horn
> of salvation.
> You promised, out of the mouths
> of the prophets long ago, that
> You would save us from
> our enemies,
> And toward our fathers
> perform mercy.
> You vowed to remember your
> covenant,
> Which you swore to our
> father, Abraham,
> that we would be delivered
> from our enemies
> and would serve you
> in holiness and righteousness
> all the days of our lives."

Zachariah darted out of the living room, burst through the middle of the astonished midwives, and to their horror grabbed his son out of the arms of Elizabeth, and rushed back into the living room. Everyone was in full agreement. Zachariah had gone quite mad.

Elizabeth edged her way to the door. What met her eyes caused her to cry, smile with delight, and be completely terrified, all at the same time.

Zachariah had raised his son high above his head and was exclaiming in a loud voice,

> "You, oh, little one,
> You will be called the *prophet*.
> The prophet of the most high God!
> You will go before the face of our
> very Lord.
> You will prepare His pathways.
> You will proclaim the kingdom
> of His salvation
> to His people,
> the remission of their sins
> by means of God's tender mercy.
> The sunrise has dawned!
> It shines on those who
> sit in darkness
> and
> in the shadow of death,
> to guide our feet
> into the way of peace."

Slowly, Zachariah lowered the child until John came to rest on the floor before his now kneeling, weeping father.

After a few moments of shocked silence, someone in the other room at last found her voice. "Zachariah! Just because you saw an angel and just because God gave you back your voice and filled you with the Holy Spirit, it does not make you a mother. You bring me back my child right now!"

17

"What do you mean, you want to go to Bethlehem with me? Augustus Caesar ordered *me* there, not you. Do you have any idea what you are saying?"

"I do, Joseph. I want to go to Bethlehem."

"Mary, in the name of sanity, you are nine months pregnant! You think you can have that baby in Bethlehem? In your condition you will very well end up having him on the side of a road. You are talking about a ninety-mile trip, hot all day, cold all night, no inns along the way, and sleeping on the roadside . . . little or no food, a worn out old donkey that may or may not be able to carry a woman that far . . . a woman who is due to give birth any minute now.

"Please, Mary, let us do it this way: Caesar's decree was just announced. We can wait.

Then, after the baby comes, I will go down to Bethlehem. That way I will miss the crowds. I may be one of the last to enroll, but as long as I get there before the date the enrollment ends, that will be good enough. In this way I can stay with you until the baby comes."

"Joseph, you are going to Bethlehem. Now. And I am going with you."

"Mary, in the name of common sense! At this moment Bethlehem is packed; I know, I grew up there. That town has only one inn, and *it* will be filled with wealthy people. Everyone else will be sleeping in the streets.

"Besides, just imagine: We start out down the road, our friends see us. Perfect strangers see us! I can hear them now. 'Greetings, sir. On your way to Bethlehem, are you? I see that as a good and caring husband you are also taking along your dear wife, who is at least ten months pregnant. And my, what a fine old donkey you have there. Why, it looks as though he can hold out for at least another mile or two. Tell me, sir, madness does not happen to run in your family, does it?'"

"Joseph, I must go to Bethlehem with you."

"Mary, please, why? What possible reasonableness can be found in such a thing?"

Mary waited. Then in a quiet, low voice she replied, "Joseph, this One who resides in my body, He is in the lineage of David; and I know that the only person who has any right to sit on David's throne must come from the house of David.''

"But you do not really know if He is going to sit on . . . "

"No, I do not. All I know is, there is that possibility. The angel said, 'and of His kingdom there will be no end.'"

"But you do *not* know *exactly* what that . . . "

"True, I do not. But just in case it means what it sounds like it means, my son is going to be born in Bethlehem."

Then, almost with a vengeance, she added, "At least no one will ever be able to cast doubt on *where* He was born."

"But what if the baby is born on the way?" Joseph argued.

"He will not be born on the way," she responded emphatically.

"Mary, you are so frustrating! You do not know that. And when we get there, are you going to be willing to sleep on the street? Are you willing to bear a child in the middle of a marketplace? Or in an alley? You cannot do that. Just where do you plan to have this child?"

"I don't know, Joseph. All I know is that we will make it to Bethlehem before He is born.

Somehow, the Lord will provide for us." As Mary finished, her eyes almost pleaded with Joseph.

"Provide for us! Provide for us! That is easy for you to say. All you have to do is have the baby. That fact cannot be changed. But I will have to live with the embarrassment of telling people 'Our son was born under a wagon out in the middle of a street. My wife insisted on it!'"

Joseph rose slowly to his feet and headed for the door.

"Where are you going?"

"Where am I going? I am going to try to figure out a way to put some extra padding on a tired old donkey so that my wife, who is at least eleven months pregnant, can have her child in a town one hundred miles from here."

"Thank you, Joseph!" Mary's tense body relaxed, and a slow smile rose to her eyes. "You are a very patient and understanding man."

For a long moment Joseph said nothing. Finally a slight smile broke upon his agitated face.

"Do not thank me, Mary. Thank that angel who keeps showing up all over the place."

18

As the young couple approached the outskirts of Bethlehem, Joseph realized he had a greater problem than even he had anticipated. Along the sides of the road, and out in the fields where shepherds were tending their flocks, were hundreds, perhaps thousands, of people. Some had erected makeshift tents, others had thrown pallets onto the ground, while yet others simply sat in the open fields.

The closer they came to Bethlehem, the more congested the road became, and the more frequent the tents and pallets and campfires of innumerable sojourners.

It was evening as they passed through the gates of the village. The scene was appalling. Every inch of the sidewalks was packed either by the mass of people or by vendors hawking their wares.

Slowly, cautiously, Joseph led the donkey through the crowded lane. At last they reached the village's only inn. A large crowd stood around the door, waiting hopelessly for someone to vacate a room. As the door swung open, Joseph caught a glimpse of the activity inside. People were standing everywhere, while a few had managed to find a place to sit on the floor. Joseph did not bother to even slow the donkey. It was obvious there was no place for them in the inn.

"I had no idea so many people had been born in Bethlehem," he muttered. "How could this little village have produced so many people?"

"Perhaps," said Mary, speaking in that mischievous tone that so disconcerted her husband, "perhaps it is because wise mothers who belong to the tribe of Judah have decided that Bethlehem is the only place for their man-child to be properly born!"

"Well . . . " Joseph sighed. "let's at least find a place to shelter the donkey for the night, and then search out a place, somewhere in this mass of humanity, where you can sleep."

Joseph looked around aimlessly for a moment, then spoke again. "There used to be a stable just at the edge of town where visitors to the inn could keep their donkeys for the night. Perhaps it is still there."

With that, the two travelers made their way down several of Bethlehem's crowded back streets until they came at last to a stable. More accurately, it was half shed and half cave. There were cows, goats, burros, one or two horses, and even several camels staked near the stable's entrance.

Joseph's face lit up when he saw the man in charge. He was a childhood friend.

Yes, the stable was filled, his friend told him. And, yes, it was impossible to shelter even one more animal there. But, yes, because of their childhood friendship, Azzan, the stable master, would take Joseph's donkey and care for it until Joseph would need it again.

The young couple made their way back toward the center of the village, looking carefully for any place to lay a pallet. Sure enough, just as they came to the corner of a congested street, two men rose from their pavement bedroom and departed into the night. Quickly Joseph spread out the blankets.

"Tonight we sleep here," he said. "And tomorrow, while I register, you will have a place to wait. It is not much, but the Lord so often gives us what we need, not what we want. Right now, He has given us a place to sleep. But He has *not* given us a place to have a baby. So do not have one until He provides for that, too!"

"It is enough," responded Mary. "On the other hand," she observed, "I would have thought the Lord's provision might have been a few inches wider."

19

Bethlehem's streets were astir early the next morning. Joseph arose with the first sounds of the village. He looked quickly about for any place that might serve more adequately for his wife and the long day's wait that lay ahead for her. There was none. The streets seemed more crowded than even his memories of yesterday. As gently as possible, he awakened Mary.

"Here are a few coins," he said. "Enough to provide you breakfast and a noon meal. I will return as soon I have finished the enrollment. I must leave now, for I have heard that the lines are long and that they move very slowly."

As expected, the day turned out to be a long and terribly dull one for Mary. There was nothing to do but to sit and to wait. Her only activity was shifting from one place on the pallet to another to best catch the shade of the day. Late in the evening

Joseph returned, obviously both angry and disappointed.

"The line is unbelievable," he growled. "Hundreds had come long before I arrived. There were only two tables set up for the enrollment. They seemed to ask every question a man could possibly know about himself and dozens he never dreamed of. At least that is what I learned from the passers-by. I never reached the officials. The whole process must begin again tomorrow. My wisest course is to stay with you until midnight, then make my way back and sleep near the two tables. That is what hundreds of others did last night. If I do the same, I should be able to have this miserable task completed by noon tomorrow."

"Joseph!" cried Mary. Her voice was filled with alarm. Joseph felt a stab of pure terror, but about what, he was not sure. "Joseph!" she cried again as she clutched his arm.

"Oh, no. Oh, no! Mary! Mary . . . you cannot have that baby right here in the streets." He helped his wife shift to another position. A wild uncertainty in Mary's eyes commanded Joseph to take some action.

"I will get the donkey. Maybe we can make it to Jerusalem before the baby comes."

"No," responded Mary firmly, not letting go of his arm. "It is too late for that. Besides, my son is to be born in Bethlehem."

"Stay here, Mary," Joseph said urgently. "I will be back in a moment. We must find a midwife and we must find a place for you to . . . to . . ." With that, Joseph jumped up, his walk soon turning to a run. Why he was going to get the donkey, he was not certain. All he knew was, he had to do something.

In a few moments he returned. "Mary, it is not a room. But there is clean hay. A bed of hay . . . my friend . . . he . . . he . . ."

"Whatever are you talking about, Joseph?" Mary asked between labored breaths, her blurred eyes blending a mixture of pain, fear, and anticipation.

"The stable. My friend has made a bed for you in the stable. He moved out our donkey, his goat, and a horse. There is room. Come. Quickly! I will look for a midwife. He told me where one lives."

Mary rose, once more clinging firmly to Joseph's arm as she stifled a sharp, hot pain.

20

The stable was dimly lit by but one small, smoky lamp. A mat of straw had been laid down near the door so that Mary might have some small relief from the foul stench of the room. Joseph's face was ashen, his entire body trembling. At this moment he could have put up a strong argument against the whole idea of reproduction.

Azzan, Joseph's lifelong (and never wed) friend, stood outside the stable, immobilized and terrified. Both men listened to the two midwives give Mary all kinds of instructions, none of which made any sense to either of them. But Joseph did hear one statement he fully understood.

"I have been a midwife for fifty years, and I have delivered thousands of babies. I am telling you, this young girl, bearing this child, is a *virgin*."

The struggle between pain and birth continued

for several hours as Mary's labor pangs came in ever shorter cycles.

Nine months earlier the Door in the heavenlies had opened into Mary's womb and there brought God into the visible creation. Now it was almost time for that same womb to open and to thereby become the entrance through which God might come forth upon this very planet.

At last, the Door opened, and like any other child ever born, He was pushed forth in harsh agony, deep red blood, and an envelope of protective water. He who had formed the world now made entrance into that world, not in the presence of trumpets and cymbals, nor in a king's palace. His reception was not as one royal born, to be arrayed in fine garments. Rather, His vestments were bands of gauze, His bed a horse's feeding trough. His lowly entrance was a dugout on the side of a hill, which some might go so far as to call a barn.

The baby cried. The mother laughed and cried. The midwives smiled in wonder at a child so strangely born. And Joseph slipped to the dirt floor and wept.

The infant's birth, except for the modest surroundings, was really no different from that of all who have abandoned the womb and entered earth's dull light. Except of course, that a giant of an angel stood just outside the stable door, poised to do battle with anything created that might have menaced this incarnation of the God of all creation.

But with the baby's first cry, Michael knew it was time to bring the good news to his kinsmen in the other realm. He hurried to this task, for he sensed that Gabriel was about to lose control of exactly one half of the heavenly host.

21

Gabriel was doing fairly well at controlling the 500 million angels in his charge. But the other 500 million, whose allegiance was to an absent Michael, were on the verge of chaos.

The excitement was understandable. This was one of the few occasions in all their long history when *all* the angels of heaven were in one place. And not since the creation of man had such numbers of angels been invited to pass through the Door onto earth in a visible form. Nonetheless, Gabriel did not want to see another total breakdown of angelic order and everything was pointing in just such a direction.

To his relief, the Door opened slightly, and Michael, his eyes ablaze with joy, stepped into the heavenlies. He raised both hands above his head, his face enraptured, his voice filled with glee.

"The child is born!"

Excitement gave way to pandemonium as every angel pressed toward the Door. Michael called for order, and though each and every angel was certain he had heartily obeyed, one would be hard pressed to actually call the scene *orderly*.

Michael looked back toward the Door in hope that it may have opened wider. It had not, but he did notice that it had moved. It seemed to have come to rest in a pasture somewhere. Michael's only thought was, "If the Door swings open in a pasture, it had better be a very large pasture, with room enough for one billion angels."

He decided to investigate. Just as he stepped onto the threshold of the Door, he was certain he heard two men having a very intense argument.

22

The place was a pasture just outside the village of Bethlehem. It was evening. The sky was clear and the stars bright. Several shepherds sat around a small fire which was dwarfed by a large boulder nearby. Two of the men, Rabof and Deruel, were, indeed, having a very animated discussion.

"Rabof, you are a stupid, illiterate shepherd. Of course angels have wings."

"You are more stupid, and more illiterate, and an even more ignorant shepherd. Angels do *not* have wings."

With this, the two men began hurling passages of Scripture at one another. When this source of information ran dry, they began, as do all men, to invent Scripture. That in turn gave way to conjecturing, reasoning, and, at last, flights of imagination that had little or nothing to do with the topic at hand.

What these shepherds did not know was that a great and mysterious portal was about to open very near them—in fact, right beside the large boulder that cast a shadow upon their tight circle. Nor could they have possibly known that at that very moment citizens of the other realm were jammed around the Door, anxious to charge through to make an announcement that was doubtlessly the greatest news ever to be proclaimed.

Sure enough, the Door did open . . . ever so slightly. Because it would be his appointed task to cross the threshold first, Gabriel peeked through the small opening.

Approximately one billion angels crammed behind Gabriel, trying to see whatever it was that met his eye. The archangel gestured for silence and for some much needed angelic self-control.

"The Door is opening upon a pasture," he observed. There was a moment's pause. "I see the village of Bethlehem in the distance!" he then exclaimed.

A moment of sheer bedlam followed as angels one and all cried out, "The city of David! The city of the King!"

Gabriel waved his hand for silence, then continued.

"There are shepherds just beyond the Door. Five of them. I cannot believe they are just sitting there! Do they not know they are but a short distance from the site of the greatest occurrence of all time and eternity?! Why do they not go into the village and see what God has . . . "

Suddenly, the Door cracked open a little more. Spontaneously Gabriel and a few others standing near him darted through the opening, while nearly one billion of their angelic kin tried desperately to follow.

Rabof, oblivious to the angelic activity, continued his debate. "You tell me just one place in Scripture or anywhere else where angels . . . uh . . . uhh . . . what is that? I mean . . . who is that? I . . . I have never seen anything like you in my whole life!"

As if out of nowhere, a giant of a creature, with a soft light glowing through his white garment, came to stand before the five shepherds. Stark terror froze them in their places.

"Why are you sitting here?" challenged Gabriel.

Not a shepherd moved.

"Why are you sitting here?" the angel repeated. "Get up! Run! Go into Bethlehem and see the wondrous thing God has done."

It was obvious to the five men that this huge creature was just about to say something else when the most phenomenal thing happened. Another of his kind appeared beside him. Then another. And then another. And yet another.

Meanwhile, in the other realm, angelic order was once more about to disintegrate. It was every angel for himself. The entire angelic host, one billion strong, was pushing its way through the Door which, mercifully, had finally opened wide.

The first angels through the Door encircled the shepherds. Those following thereafter filled the immediate surroundings, careful always not to step on any of the sheep. A few of the angels ascended the towering boulder.

Still the citizens of the heavenlies poured through the Door. Soon the white-robed visitors had filled the entire pasture land. On they came. Innumerable. Now the hills surrounding the pastures were filled.

And yet came more, until it seemed every inch of earth from the hills surrounding Bethlehem to the outskirts of Jerusalem were filled with messengers from heaven. They were everywhere, as far as shepherds' eyes could see. Mile upon mile the pastures and hills glowed with the light of these luminous creatures.

As the angels themselves began to take in the magnificence of this unprecedented sight, they each began to shout with uninhibited joy. Pandemonium and delight wed in an exquisite moment of rapture. The sound was like a roar of a thousand seas. But as the discordant shouts of joy billowed forth, they began to change and become one colossal anthem of adoration and praise.

> "Glory, glory, glory.
> Glory to God!
> Glory to God who is
> in the highest. And here on earth,
> peace!
> Peace has come among men
> with whom He is pleased."

The shepherds, left with no other choice, fell on their faces, stunned by the glory of their surroundings.

On and on the angels sang. Dumbfounded shepherds, finally adjusting to the impossible, rose to their feet and quite spontaneously joined in the chorus, though they still had no idea what it was they rejoiced in, and cared even less. After all, in the midst of such a scene, anything less than full-throated praise was simply unthinkable.

Still, the shepherds could not but wonder, "What on earth is this? A sudden sea of strange beings. Who are these creatures with the glories of heaven on their faces and in their song? What are they doing *here?*"

Once more Gabriel called out to the shepherds, but this time his hand pointed straight at them and his voice left no room for debate. *This* was a command!

"Why are you standing here? Go into the city of David and see what God has done!"

It was half out of fear and half out of obedience that the five men struck out for Bethlehem. Their path, of course, led them straight through the angelic host. But eventually they found their way to the open road and, for inexplicable reasons, ran toward a barn on the outskirts of Bethlehem.

A few moments later one billion angels returned to their own habitat, there to continue their glorious anthem. But as the last angel passed through the Door, he noticed that it did not entirely close. A ray of light from the brightness of the glory of heaven seeped through that small opening and poured out into the visible realm.

The angel also noticed that the Door began to move again. If he was not mistaken, it was moving eastward. Could he possibly trust his eyes? Beneath the sky and clouds . . . surely not! Was that not Babylon he saw?

And why, he wondered, was the Door left slightly ajar? If that really was Babylon down there, and if the light of heaven really was seeping through the doorway into the skies above Babylon, surely such a thing would cause a great consternation in the city below.

And what of our two argumentative shepherds? They at last came to the entrance to the stable. Just before entering they stopped to catch their breath. At that point, one turned to the other and spoke.

"Rabof, I apologize. You were right; I was wrong. Angels do not have wings!"

23

It was still dark when Mary, Joseph and the child departed Bethlehem for Jerusalem. It was now the fortieth day since Jesus' birth. By Levitical law today was Jesus' day of dedication and Mary's day for purification at the temple.

Joseph had a pressing concern, the dangers facing them on the highway. The morning trek to Jerusalem would be safe enough, but they would not be returning to Bethlehem until that evening, a dangerous time to be on the road because of robbers and highwaymen. Perhaps they should spend the night with kinsmen in Jerusalem. It was a long trip for a mother; using the old donkey as transportation was out of the question. She had to walk, both directions. Breaking the trip up into a two-day journey seemed wise. On the other hand, he needed sorely to be back at his carpentry shop early on the morrow.

As day broke and Jerusalem's walls appeared in the distance, Joseph's mind began to wander back to a vivid childhood memory. Gradually, as he became lost in thought, he unwittingly had also become very silent. So much so that it was beginning to bother Mary. She moved in front of him, stopped, turned and faced him.

"What are you thinking?"

So absorbed had Joseph been in his thoughts, and so abrupt was this unexpected intrusion, that he had to pause and ask himself the same question.

"I have been thinking of an elderly lady. I used to walk over to Jerusalem from Bethlehem a lot when I was a boy, usually during one of the festivals. Some of us children played on the temple steps and among its many outer corridors. Well, we often saw a very old woman there. We were told that she almost literally lived in the temple. She was praying for the coming of the Messiah."

Joseph was not sure what to say next, or if he should say anything at all. But a further explanation to Mary was not necessary. For a long time they walked in silence.

"Is she still alive?" asked Mary pensively.

"I was wondering the same thing. I sincerely doubt it. By now she would be ancient."

Again the couple fell silent. Joseph found himself turning one question over and over again in his mind. If she were still alive, and if she saw this child, a child around whom so many strange things had occurred, what might be her reaction?

"Joseph, is there any chance at all that she is still alive?"

"None, Mary. Even when I was a little boy, it seemed every day was her last. She was as aged as any human I have ever laid eyes upon. And that was nearly fifteen years ago. But I do wish she might have lived."

But even as Joseph spoke these words, the face of that ancient woman hounded his thoughts. He recalled her high, thin voice, the maze of wrinkles on her face, and that obscure place where she always went to pray. Could he find that place again? Perhaps later in the day he could find someone in the temple who would remember her. Maybe they could tell him what had finally happened to that strange old woman who had prayed so many years for the birth of the Messiah.

"If she were alive," thought Joseph, "and if she saw this child, and if she said anything special about him . . . I would never doubt anything again as long as I lived!"

24

The young couple arrived at the temple just in time for the beginning of the rites of dedication for all the children born forty days ago.

When this ceremony was over, the rite of purification began. Joseph dismissed himself so that he might purchase two turtle doves or two pigeons to be offered on the altar before they departed the temple.

Joseph bent down and whispered to Mary, "I will go now and exchange some of our good Galileen money for temple money and purchase our offering. I will return shortly. While I am at the exchange table I will try to find someone who may remember the old prophetess. I have been trying to remember her name. I think it was Hanna or Ann or Anna."

Buying the turtle doves took longer than he had

anticipated, but he decided to take a few moments to wander around the temple, nonetheless. He had no sooner begun his search for word of the old prophetess than he came upon his wife and baby. Mary had been inquiring, too.

Together the young couple wandered about from portico to portico, being especially careful to look in the shadows. They were about to end their search when Joseph spotted a particular dark corner behind one of the porticos. "That is the place," said Joseph softly. Reverently the two approached the shadowy area.

"There is no one here, Mary. I am sorry. It has simply been too long. She could not have possibly lived for so long a time."

Mary sat down upon the base of a pillar and began gently rocking her baby. She was very tired. A melancholy look was upon her face. It had been a long, hard morning, and the early morning walk from Bethlehem had taken its toll.

The quiet was broken by a high-pitched, ancient, but almost childlike, voice. Joseph recognized it instantly.

"The baby . . . that baby . . . whose baby is that?" An old woman suddenly appeared from seemingly nowhere. "That is *the* baby! That is the child I have waited for so long . . . oh, so long."

The ancient form knelt beside Mary and carefully opened the covers around the baby's face.

"My child," she said, looking into Mary's face. "Do you know who this is? This baby? He is the Messiah!"

The old one then looked up toward Joseph, her eyesight obviously very dim. Almost as a child might, she spoke again.

"I have come here every day. I often sleep here. Young man, do you know this baby? Do you know who it is?"

Mary began shaking. She was obviously trying to hold back some deep, traumatic emotion, but she was not faring well in her efforts. The old woman reached up and pulled back Mary's headcovering.

"You are but a young girl."

Hot tears poured down Mary's face.

The elderly woman looked into her eyes compassionately. "You . . . you are a virgin, are you not?"

With that, Mary's emotions tore loose from their moorings. She flung her arms around the prophetess and buried her face in her aged neck. This desperate act was followed by a torrent of tears and uncontrollable sobs. Mary's entire body began to tremble.

Doubts and fears about the events of this last year had chosen this moment to surface.

Joseph had never seen Mary like this. This strong, dauntless girl who had stood courageously throughout all the events of this past year, had at last crumbled. Joseph felt overwhelmed with sadness, yet at the same time incredibly proud of this wondrous young woman he called his wife.

The old prophetess addressed Joseph again. "She is a virgin, is she not? She must be a virgin."

Before Joseph could answer, Mary lifted her head and tried to speak. But only by the greatest exertion of will could she manage to utter even one word. That she wanted so desperately to be the one to answer the question was obvious, but whether or not she could do so remained in serious doubt.

Mary sat up, wiped her tears and tried once more to gain control of her emotions. But each time she struggled to speak even one word she would again be overcome by sobs.

"I . . . I . . . " Mary seemed determined to make some declaration. Still the tears refused to subside. Then, despite the sobs, despite the violent trembling of her body, Mary began a pronouncement intended for the whole world, the principalities and the powers, the thrones and dominions.

"Yes . . . I . . . am! Yes, I am . . . a virgin! I am! I am a virgin!"

Again Mary burst into deep, convulsive sobs.

After a moment, she continued.

"I am. But, dear lady. Oh, dear lady, I never really knew anybody in the world would know that for sure! How did you know? Dear lady, how did you know?"

"Because Isaiah said it would be that way," the old woman replied gently. "Have you never heard of Isaiah, dear one?"

Once more Mary lost complete control of herself. But this time her sobs were intermingled with tiny cries of joy.

"Yes. Yes," she said. "I have heard of Isaiah. I know what Isaiah said . . ."

Once more Mary convulsed with unrestrained sobs. But again she forced herself to sit up and wipe her tears.

"Dear lady," she said, trying to look into the old woman's face. "Can you imagine how difficult . . . do you . . . realize . . . what it is . . . like?" Mary again buried her face in the old woman's arms.

After a long time of weeping, punctuated again and again by struggles to regain her composure, Mary managed to continue. "I . . . could . . . never . . . fully believe . . . " Again Mary had to stop. It seemed her heart would surely burst as she struggled to finish.

"I . . . was . . . never . . . quite sure . . . Isaiah was. . . "

With the end of her sentence finally in sight, Mary released one last cataract of tears, her words mingled in between gasps for air.

"I was never sure . . . it was so hard to believe . . . that Isaiah was talking about . . . about *me!*"

The old woman smiled as she brought Mary to her bosom and cradled her head in her wrinkled hands.

Joseph extended one arm, gently laying his hand on Mary's shoulder, and knelt beside the old lady. His own face was now a river of tears.

"Your name is Anna, is it not?" asked Joseph. "I saw you many times here when I was a boy. My friends and I often came from Bethlehem to play around the temple grounds on holidays."

Searching Joseph's face with her tired eyes, the old lady responded cheerfully, "And you grew up to be a fine young man." Then she turned her eyes back to the teen-age girl who was softly weeping in her arms.

"You must be a most remarkable girl. And God has given you a fine young man for a husband."

The young couple reached out to one another, and Joseph joined Mary in a chorus of sobs and tears, more of laughter now than of pain.

Anna once again peered into the face of the infant. She spoke several words to Him in some ancient, long-forgotten Hebrew dialect, then reached over and kissed Mary. With that, she raised a hand to Joseph, who carefully lifted the venerable old woman to her feet.

"I am going into the temple now," spoke the weary but still childlike voice.

Slowly, as in a cadence, she spoke again, pausing briefly after each word. "I am going to tell everyone what I have seen. I have come here every day of my life for so many years. I have prayed night and day. I have fasted for so long. I have waited for so long."

She stopped, then Anna raised her face toward the heavens. The glory of God rested upon it.

"I do not have to come here any more," she said softly. "I am going into the temple to tell everyone I do not have to come here any more. And when I have told everyone that I do not have to come here any more, I am going to go home. And I am going to go to bed, and God is going to send His angels to carry me to His bosom."

The old prophetess began to move down the hall, her voice finally trailing off until it was but an echo among the corridors.

For a long time Joseph and Mary stood watching as Anna disappeared from view. The noonday sun broke forth through one of the temple's portals, bending its rays down around the young couple.

After a long moment, Joseph turned to Mary and said, "Let us go now and make our offering. It is a long way home, and we must start back."

"Should we not spend the night here," Mary replied, "and wait to travel tomorrow? You have been so concerned for me. What of the heat, the distance, the possibility of robbers so late in the day?"

"It is all right," Joseph replied matter-of-factly. "Our Lord is going to take care of us. He really, really is."

25

Caspin made his long midnight climb from the city of Babylon up to the crest of Mount Atar. There he would do what he had faithfully done for so many years, to record the position of the stars.

Caspin's order, the order of the Magi, had built a marble wall upon this mountaintop, and all along the wall were measuring instruments set there to track the movement of the stellar bodies. As Caspin moved along the wall, he carefully aligned each instrument, took measurements, and dutifully recorded his findings.

Caspin was just about to write something in one of the ancient books when he thought his peripheral vision had caught a glimpse of . . . of what? A comet? A falling meteor? He glanced up. What was *that?* He had never seen anything like it. Instinctively he repositioned a number of the instruments to line up with this strange celestial visitor.

"This is not a star," Caspin mused to himself. "This is not a comet. What is it? It does not belong where it is. And unless I am going clean mad, it does not appear that far distant from me."

Throughout the long night, Caspin checked his instruments and searched the records of ancient books. At last he decided to do something he had never done before. He would go down into the city, awaken others of the Magi, and reveal to them his findings. He only hoped that *thing* out there would not disappear.

Hurriedly Caspin made his way down the narrow trail into the city and to the door of one of his faithful friends.

"Call me mad if you wish," Caspin said to Akard, "but get up and get dressed. It is still there, see for yourself." Caspin nudged his friend to the open window. "There, right up there."

Akard rubbed his eyes, looked into the sky, looked back into the face of Caspin and, without a word, began putting on his robes. "Go get Gazerim. Awaken the whole order if necessary," he muttered.

Within the hour, over half of the order of the Magi were atop Mount Atar checking instruments, making notes, and feverishly consulting with one another, about what, they were not sure.

Finally Caspin spoke: "There is nothing more we can do here tonight. Tomorrow evening some of us must gather here again. Others of us must ascend to the highest mountain we can find to the east, and yet others must climb to the top of the mountains to the west. For myself, I am leaving immediately for the south."

"The *south?*" exclaimed Gazerim. "Why the south? Measurements are only necessary from three sides."

"Because," said Caspin, "because . . . no, I dare not say."

"You will say. It is your duty to speak. There has never been a phenomenon like this. It is our sworn duty to watch the heavens for any sign the gods may send to us."

Caspin looked up toward the shiny new star. Only his fingering of the leaves of one of the ancient books betrayed the anxious wonder within him. Dare he utter what he believed? After a long pause, he spoke.

"I will tell you what I am thinking, but you must promise to call me neither mad nor a fool; and you must promise not to remove me from the order of the Magi for what I am about to say."

The others solemnly responded with an oath.

"I believe," said Caspin firmly, "that this star is not far distant from us. It hangs in the sky just beyond our city. As I move southward, I will take measurements. I believe I can succeed in getting *beyond* that star. If so, we can know not only if it is moving, but also in what direction it moves. We may be able, after a few nights, to plot its speed. With good fortune we may be able to . . . to tell the actual distance this fiery phenomenon is from us.''

"You plan to travel to the *other side* of a star? You are mad!" cried one of the Magi, but the withering glare of the rest of his order caused him to drop his head. Without a word of response, Caspin started down the mountain.

A week later the entire order of the Magi had been called together (by no less than the revered Rab-Magi) to hear an incredible report from the returning Caspin.

"I traveled south a full three days' journey. By the third day, my horse had taken me *beyond* the star. I turned. The star was now north of me. Its position fell halfway between me and the southern portion of the city of Babylon. Fellow Magi, that star, or whatever it is, lies about halfway between Mount Atar and the southern desert."

"Are you certain?" asked Gazerim.

"More certain than I am of life itself."

A long discussion followed. Questions were asked. Heads shook. Tempers flared. Then Caspin spoke again.

"Our task is threefold. First we must compare

your nightly plottings with those I configurated while I was away. We must plot the direction of this strange star. The gods are telling us something. Whatever it is, we dare not misunderstand it.

"Second, if at all possible, we must do something that no man has ever done before. We must calculate and configure until we discover at what time in past history the stars were aligned in the sky exactly as they are tonight."

"It cannot be done!" exclaimed one of the Magi.

"You are correct, it cannot be done," responded Gazerim gruffly. "But we must try, anyway. The gods are watching."

"What is the third thing?" asked Akard.

"We must search out every ancient writing, every book, every document. We must find every prophecy ever given that might be connected with what it is we see in the sky."

"That could take months, even years," protested one of the Magi.

Gazerim stood and addressed the order: "Fellow Magi, if it takes our lifetime, we must do exactly what Caspin has said. This is the very purpose of our order. There has never been a phenomenon like this. Therefore, we can assume there has never been an event foretold by the stars that is as important as this one."

"Shall a vote be taken?" asked Caspin.

"No," responded the Rab-Magi. "What Gazerim has said is true. We have only one task until this riddle is solved."

Caspin nodded. "Then let us be to it."

26

For weeks the Magi poured over long columns of mathematical figures, seeking to discover the last time the stars had been in this position. Still others went through all the ancient books kept by their own order, all the libraries of Babylon, and sacred texts that had been stored in mountain caves for centuries. Finally they searched out the records of the palace—as far back as the writings of Darius and Cyrus.

Months passed as the Magi continued their feverish research. Still the riddle would not give.

Then one day Akard announced a meeting. Once more the entire order assembled.

"We have not been able to discern the last time the stars were in this position," he said. "But some among us believe it was approximately one thousand years ago. Nonetheless, we cannot be certain.

"Among all the ancient writings, we have found perhaps five prophecies that may possibly refer to this star. Of these, none is a certainty. But yesterday I visited a Hebrew rabbi; he is one of the leaders of those Jews who still live among us. Quite frankly, he was not all that helpful, but he did remember that long ago one who belonged to our own order had made a prophecy. A strange prophecy it was, during the days when the Hebrews were held captive among us. The rabbi assured me that this prophecy was recorded not only in our writings but also in their own sacred text. He suggested that someone in our order try to interpret this mysterious prophecy. I would have paid little attention to what the man said, except that all the calculations we have made concerning the path of this star indicate that it is slowly, but relentlessly, moving in a direction that will take it over the city of Jerusalem."

"What is the prophecy?" asked Caspin.

"It has to do with weeks of years, or something of that nature; I am not sure. It can be found in the records of the Magi during the period of the golden age of Babylon. It is also recorded in one of their own books penned by a prophet named Daniel."

For the next few weeks the Magi minutely examined every word of the ancient prophecy.

There were many interpretations, but there was one that troubled them more than any other. If this interpretation proved to be correct, it meant some great event was taking place, at that very moment, in Israel.

"Among the Hebrews?" each mused. "Why not among the Babylonians?"

"We really have no choice, do we?" declared Akard. "The star moves inexorably toward the west. It will soon be out of our line of vision. If our calculations are correct, it moves toward the capital city of Israel. It would appear that in this very year, some new king is being born—a king who is a descendant of their original king. The rabbi, to whom I now speak frequently, assures me that it would have to be someone who is a descendant of a king they most love and venerate. His name was David."

"The star of the house of David?" asked Caspin to himself.

"If these things be true," said the Rab-Magi, rising to his feet, "then we must conclude that this is the greatest sign that will be given in our lifetime. The sign of a king. A great king. Perhaps a delivering king, born in Jerusalem. We must send messengers to their ruler and inquire about a son. And we must pay homage to him, lest we displease the gods who have so favored us with this sign."

"Who shall go?" one of the Magi inquired.

"Caspin, by all means. And Akard, who has broken the riddle." All nodded in agreement. Then came another voice, "And Gazerim, who has been so bullheaded." Everyone laughed in approval.

"And what shall we send as gifts?" asked Gazerim.

"We shall send gold," said Caspin. With that word, everyone cheered. "And frankincense!" cried another. Once more the selection pleased the Magi. The oldest of the order rose and said solemnly, "And perhaps, we must send myrrh." There was a long silence. Then one after another, the Magi nodded in agreement.

Caspin rose, "So be it. We shall leave with tomorrow's dawn. The star is growing quite distant to our eyes."

27

Cautiously Mary cracked open the door just wide enough to get a better look at the men standing at her door. "Just a moment, please."

With these words Mary closed the door, pushed it firmly shut, fastened the latch, turned and ran through the house, out the back door, and down the alley to the nearby carpentry shop where Joseph was working.

"Joseph, come with me immediately."

"What is it?"

"Do not ask, just come. You would not believe me anyway," she said, as she pushed him out the door. "I do not believe it, and I saw it."

Together the couple rushed back up the alley, into their small house, and to the front door.

Mary cracked open the door once more. There

before her stood three tall, swarthy-looking men. Neither she nor Joseph had ever seen such odd-looking people.

"My name is Caspin," said the tallest stranger.

"Yes, I know. You told me that," replied Mary. "You are an astrologer?"

"Well . . ." Caspin began.

"You are a Babylonian?" continued Mary.

"Yes, we have come from Babylon."

Mary cast a wary look at the tall stranger. "You are an astrologer, and you are a Babylonian? And you want to see *my* baby?"

Akard approached the door, "Madam."

"Who are you?"

"My name is Akard."

"Why would a Babylonian astrologer want to see my baby?" asked Mary menacingly.

"It is because of the star. It appeared to us over Babylon. The star of . . . we believe it to be the star of David, your ancient and venerable king."

"A star," said Mary. "You Babylonian astrologers have seen a star? Do you not know our religion prohibits us from having anything to do with astrologers?"

With that, Gazerim stepped up. "Dear lady, we

are not exactly astrologers. We are an ancient order that counsels our kings. Mostly we interpret dreams."

"You have dreams as well as stars?" asked Mary, still holding the door almost shut.

Gazerim cleared his throat, "No, dear lady. We have had no dreams. We interpret dreams for our kings so that they might understand what it is the gods, uh . . . what it is God is telling them. It was one such dream that set your people free from their captivity in Babylon."

"Oh," replied Mary, as she opened the door just a little.

Gazerim continued, "We study the stars to see if there are signs in the heavens. In fact, it has been centuries since there has been any truly great sign in the heavens."

Akard spoke again, "Even your prophets speak of signs in the heavens, you know."

Mary opened the door a little further.

Gazerim moved forward a step. "Several months ago a star appeared over our city. We calculated its direction. It was moving toward Jerusalem, or so we thought. Therefore, we traveled from our land to yours, arriving in Jerusalem just yesterday. Last night the star appeared again over your village, Bethlehem."

Caspin interrupted, "Where your ancient and

much loved king was born. David, the great king. The good king. He was born here. You are aware of this?"

"Yes," replied Mary.

"And are you one of his descendants?"

"I am," said Mary as she pulled the door open wider. "And so is my husband. We are both in direct and unbroken lineage to King David."

With an edge of excitement in his voice, Caspin asked, "And have you birthed a child? A male child?"

Mary stared at the three men for a long time.

"Why do you want to know?" she queried.

"Because the heavens indicate that a great king, perhaps the greatest of all kings, has been born here in Bethlehem."

Joseph began to shake his head and mutter, "Yet once more . . . the unbelievable. This time it is Babylonian, heathen, gentile astrologers!"

"I have a son," Mary began slowly. "He was born to me in the most unusual of circumstances. There was an angel and . . . " Mary paused.
" . . . and other things surrounding his birth that were even more amazing. There were the shepherds who came on the night he was born. They told of seeing a great host of angels standing in the fields just outside our village.

"And then there was an ancient woman at the temple in Jerusalem, her name was Anna; she had spent her whole life waiting for the Messiah."

"The Messiah!" cried Caspin, almost dropping something he was holding in his arms. "Never in all my thoughts! The Messiah!"

Gazerim dropped to his knees, as did Akard. "We implore you, kind lady, let us see this child. Let us adore Him and worship Him. We have brought gifts to Him."

"But are you not gentiles?" asked Mary. She looked up at Joseph, her face reflecting her puzzlement. Joseph shrugged his shoulders, took a deep breath, laughed, and said, "Why not? Even a heathen, gentile astrologer from Babylon has certain rights, I suppose. If our God has seen fit to make known to them these wondrous things, who are we to question it?"

Mary peered intently at the men one more time.

"You won't hurt my baby, will you?"

"The gods forbid it!" responded Akard in alarm. Mary hesitated, then motioned for the men to come inside.

"He is in the kitchen where I have been cooking a meal. His name is Jesus. His name means 'God will save His people.'"

Reverently the three men approached the child.

As they did, Akard turned to Gazerim in blank wonder. "The Messiah is in the kitchen!"

Gazerim smiled and shook his head.

Mary did not hear their words, but her own thoughts were similar. "How strange," she mused. "Three heathen have traveled hundreds of miles, only to end their search and their journey in my kitchen."

Joseph, in turn, had his own thoughts. "Uncircumcised, idol worshiping, heathen, Babylonian, gentile, magician-astrologers, "come to worship our little boy. What manner of child must this be."

28

The young couple accompanied the three Magi to the barn where they had earlier stabled their camels.

"You are sure it is all right if we keep the gold and the myrrh and the frankincense?" asked Mary incredulously.

"They are small gifts for so great a king," assured Caspin.

"Well, you could stay the night," said Joseph. "There is an inn here in our village. And it is not crowded. In fact," he added with a grin, "I do not recall its being filled for over a year now."

"No," replied Gazerim as he mounted his camel. "We must return to Jerusalem with this great news. There are those waiting to hear."

"What do you mean?" asked Mary.

"We have promised to report back to the wise men of your religion, the ones who told us of the prophecy that the great king would be born here in this village."

"And more," said Akard. "Yesterday it was our privilege to meet your present king. He was very pleased to know that there might be one born of equal greatness to himself. He asked us to return to him and tell him if we found the child who was born under David's star."

Joseph looked up into the face of Akard, "You met Herod the Great? He knows of the birth of our son?"

"Yes," said Akard. "We met him in his own palace. He was quite warm and hospitable. And he was very excited about the news."

Mary's face grew ashen. Joseph spoke, his words direct and strong.

"Before you return to speak to the king and to our leaders, would you first ask our God for wisdom? It may be that our Lord would have the birth of this child be kept secret for a while longer."

The three men exchanged glances and then nodded in assent. Before mounting his camel, Caspin walked over to Mary and planted a kiss on the forehead of the young boy she held in her arms. He then added a blessing in his heathen tongue.

As they rode off, Joseph wondered out loud, "What does this mean?" Mary crossed her arms as if to ward off a sudden chill. "Can it mean . . ." The sentence remained unfinished.

Joseph completed the sentence, saying what they both were thinking. " . . . that the gentiles will come to worship Him just as much as may His own people?"

They made the short walk back to their small home in silence. As they arrived at the door, Mary revealed her anxious thoughts. "Herod . . . he knows. This is *not* good."

"Not good at all," agreed Joseph.

"Joseph, please, what shall we do? I am very uneasy. In fact, I am worried. That wicked man in Jerusalem is the most evil creature who ever lived. He wishes nothing good for our child."

Joseph put his arm around Mary and led her into the house. Long into the night the young couple shared their thoughts about what they might do; but unable to come to any conclusion, they at last fell asleep. A few moments later, the Door from the other realm opened into the small living room where the young couple and their child lay sleeping.

Gabriel knelt beside Joseph and stared into the young carpenter's face. Joseph turned restlessly. Gabriel did not move. Rather, he continued his motionless vigil. At last the archangel touched

Joseph's forehead. Then, standing, he stepped back through the Door.

Joseph awoke with a start.

"Mary!" he cried. "A dream. I have had another dream! We must leave here immediately. It is some dreadful thing. Some monstrous evil. Herod will seek the life of our child. I know the dream is true. It was that same angel who appeared to me before. I saw him!"

Joseph sat up and turned toward Mary. "You are not going to like this, but I dare not disobey. The angel told me that we must take the baby out of Judea."

"Oh, Joseph, another move? Please, Joseph, not Nazareth."

"Mary, I told you, you are not going to like this. We are to go into *Egypt.*"

"Egypt!" cried Mary. "Never! They worship bugs in Egypt!"

"Mary, we are not going to disobey the very angel who appeared to you, and who also has this odd habit of haunting *my* sleep. We are going to Egypt. We must. In the dream I heard the wail of thousands of mothers. I felt the death of little children all over our land."

Mary sat up, "The gold. This is why God sent us the gold. I knew we were not supposed to be rich. We are to use the gold to flee into Egypt."

Mary threw off the covers, speaking in an unbroken stream of words as she did. "We must leave immediately. Tonight. Joseph, wake that friend of yours, the owner of the stable. You know, Azzan. Buy a camel. We will use the camel for carrying our belongings and food and water. And buy a new donkey. A young, strong donkey. That floppy eared old donkey of yours will never make it to Egypt."

"What about all those bugs?" replied Joseph good-naturedly, still savoring the fact he had so quickly won this one.

"Joseph," responded Mary thoughtfully, ignoring his last remark, "there is something else we must do. The wrath of Satan has been kindled against our child, and the Lord has delivered us. But there are two children involved here. John is in as much danger as is Jesus. We must go to Elizabeth and Zachariah and warn them of the danger their child faces. They *must* go with us to Egypt."

"No, Mary, I forbid it. We do not have time. Every minute puts our son at greater risk. I will send Zachariah and Elizabeth some of our gold. I will send it by one of my trusted kinsmen, along with a letter. The three of them can flee, perhaps, into the wilderness. There they can hide among the Essenes or some of the nomads. Herod's forces will never be able to cover all of the southern wastelands. That is as much as we dare to do. We

125

must believe that the Lord will take care of John, just as He is taking care of our son."

That night the young couple bought a camel they laughingly named Pharoah, and the largest, strongest donkey they had ever seen, named Bashan. At dawn Joseph and Mary took Jesus and began their flight across the Sinai desert and into the land where men did, indeed, worship bugs.

It would be of Egypt that the young child, Jesus, would have His earliest memories. Nor would He forget that among the first things He ever learned was that He was a fugitive and a wayfarer upon this earthen ball.

29

Out of Egypt they came, having heard of the death of Herod and having also received assurance in a dream that it was safe now to bring their son back to the land of Israel. Nonetheless, the journey across the desert was as miserable in returning as it had been in going.

Each night they slept under the stars, while by day their travel was confined to only the early morning and late evening. The larger part of each day was spent hiding in the shadow of a rock from the sun's blistering rays.

After weeks of this wretched trek, Mary, the young lad Jesus, and Joseph caught their first sight of the fertile hills of Judea.

Mary eagerly told her son every particular she could think of concerning his homeland, his cousin, John (whom she hoped he would soon meet), and their other kin. Mary still held the hope in her heart that she would raise Jesus in Bethlehem. Surely now, with the wicked Herod dead, they would be able to settle in Judea.

Having come to an inn just within the borders of Israel, the exhausted family enjoyed their first night's rest in over two years in the land of their own people.

The innkeeper told them all the details of the mass murder Herod had ordered of all the baby boys in and around Bethlehem. The news of Herod's death had filled the entire nation with relief and joy. But when Joseph and Mary heard that a son of Herod, Archelaus, reigned over Judea, they were once again filled with anxiety. And again they found themselves talking far into the night.

Mary still held out some vague hope of being able to return to Bethlehem. Joseph insisted on Galilee.

Mary winced. "If we go to Galilee," she replied, "I have one request, that we not live in Nazareth."

"Mary, I had a promising business in Nazareth just three years ago. I gave up that business, closed the shop, and started all over again in Bethlehem so our son could be raised in the city of David. Then we had to give that up for Egypt! For the two years we lived there we hardly met a person to whom we could even speak. Now the gold is almost gone. We have just enough money to start over again."

"But Joseph," Mary interrupted, "why must we start over again back where we came from? Why Nazareth?"

Joseph continued, "Judea is ruled by a man who has the blood of Herod coursing through his veins. But Galilee is free of that dark shadow. I can reopen my shop in Nazareth the day I arrive there. Soon I will have a good business going. And when our son is a little older, he will be able to help. Furthermore . . . "

"Joseph," Mary stopped him again. "Do you not know the old saying, 'Can anything good come out of Nazareth?' I can hardly bear to think of raising our precious boy in such a dishonorable town. Most of the people in Nazareth are gentiles. The Romans have a garrison stationed there. The streets are filthy. People are poor. Most of all, there is a meanness to that place."

"Mary, are you willing to risk raising Jesus in Bethlehem?"

"No, His life may be at risk there. No, I dare not. Not after what Herod did to the children of Judea. It frightens me just to think that a kinsman of Herod rules from his throne. I have only asked that if we move to Galilee we do not live in Nazareth."

"We have until tomorrow to decide," replied

Joseph, not eager to make the final decision on a matter about which they both felt so strongly. "Tomorrow we must take the road that leads to Judea or the road that leads to Galilee. Perhaps in the morning it will be clear to both of us which direction we should go."

Soon after the young couple fell asleep, Gabriel slipped through the Door for what would be his last visit to either Mary or Joseph. Soon the young boy would become keenly conscious that His Father lived within Him. When He grew to know His indwelling Father perfectly, there would be no need for angelic visitations. He would, of Himself, perceive the invisible realm. The Father and the Son would fellowship with one another, spirit to spirit.

Gabriel knelt down before Joseph and spoke to him for the last time.

"You must not go into Judea. The child is still in danger. Go. Return to Galilee, to Nazareth, and make your home there."

Gabriel stood, gazing for a long time at the carpenter, his wife, and the incredible young boy who slept beside them. This heavenly visitor knew that in the not-too-distant future all his allegiance would be wholly to this child, this Son of the Living God, who bore the earthly name Jesus.

Gabriel began to move toward the Door. But just before he stepped through the portal, he returned and knelt before his sovereign Lord.

30

"What can I say?" said Mary. "The angel who first appeared to you in a dream saved our marriage. That same angel appeared to you in another dream and saved the life of our son from sure destruction. Now that self-same angel has spoken to us once again. We are to go to Galilee. But I cannot tell you that I consider this to be good news. Joseph, are you certain that we must return to that mean and miserable town, Nazareth?"

"Yes, Mary, I am certain."

Joseph took his wife in his arms and lifted her upon the strong, sturdy donkey. He reached down and picked up the boy and balanced him on his strong right arm.

The innkeeper stepped out into the sunlight and

asked the young couple if they had decided to go to Judea.

"No," replied Joseph, "We are going to Galilee." With that, Joseph began leading the donkey slowly down the road.

"And where in Galilee will you live?" called out the innkeeper. "In Nazareth," shouted Joseph.

The innkeeper cupped his hands to his mouth and yelled out, "Can anything good come out of Nazareth?"

Mary turned her head abruptly, and cried in a loud, clear voice, "Yes, there is something *wonderful* that will come out of Nazareth."

"My Son!"

By Gene Edwards

The Birth

The Divine Romance

A Tale of Three Kings

The Revolution (Part I)

The Secret to the Christian Life

The Highest Life

The Inward Journey

Letters to a Devastated Christian

Our Mission

Preventing a Church Split

Gene Edwards is one of the foremost Christian story tellers of this day. He is a retired Southern Baptist minister who served as a pastor and evangelist before entering upon a 25-year ministry on the deeper Christian life. His pen now renders some of the deepest truths of the Christian faith into the simplest of stories.

Edwards holds a B.A. in English literature and history from East Texas State University, with a master of theology from Southwestern Baptist Theological Seminary, and presently makes his home in New England. *The Birth* is the first installment of an epic, to be followed by *The Beginning, The Life, The Resurrection,* and *The Return.* He is also in the process of completing a saga of the first century believer entitled The Revolution.

If you have enjoyed *The Birth,* you will equally enjoy Edwards' other two books written in a similar genre: *The Divine Romance* and *A Tale of Three Kings.*

The Birth was typeset in 12-point Times Romans by Pinetree Composition, Lewiston, Maine, printed by Bookcrafters of Chelsea, Michigan, on acid-free 50-lb., antique white paper, and published by The Seed Sowers of Auburn, Maine. The cover design is by Albert Tomlinson of Auburn, Maine.